Cowboy Camp

Tammi Sauer

Illustrated by
Mike Reed

Sterling Publishing Co., Inc.
New York

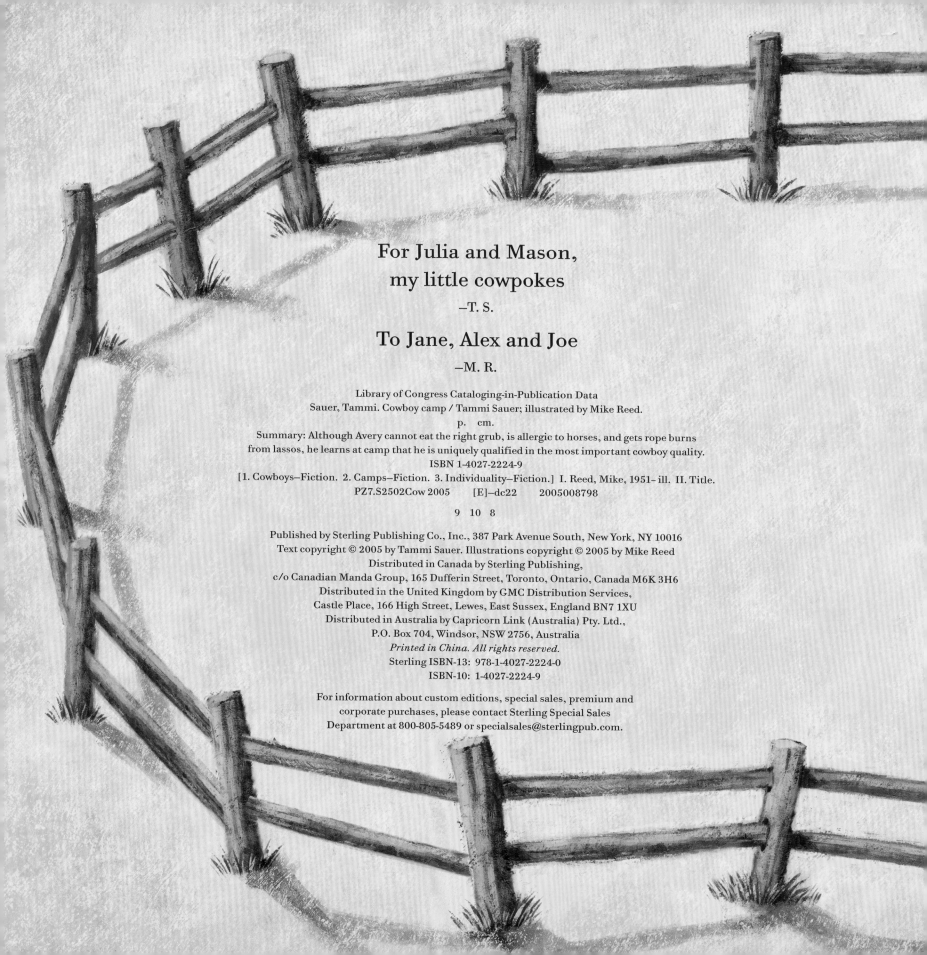

For Julia and Mason,
my little cowpokes

–T. S.

To Jane, Alex and Joe

–M. R.

Library of Congress Cataloging-in-Publication Data
Sauer, Tammi. Cowboy camp / Tammi Sauer; illustrated by Mike Reed.
p.   cm.
Summary: Although Avery cannot eat the right grub, is allergic to horses, and gets rope burns
from lassos, he learns at camp that he is uniquely qualified in the most important cowboy quality.
ISBN 1-4027-2224-9
[1. Cowboys–Fiction. 2. Camps–Fiction. 3. Individuality–Fiction.] I. Reed, Mike, 1951– ill. II. Title.
PZ7.S2502Cow 2005   [E]–dc22   2005008798

9   10   8

Published by Sterling Publishing Co., Inc., 387 Park Avenue South, New York, NY 10016
Text copyright © 2005 by Tammi Sauer. Illustrations copyright © 2005 by Mike Reed
Distributed in Canada by Sterling Publishing,
c/o Canadian Manda Group, 165 Dufferin Street, Toronto, Ontario, Canada M6K 3H6
Distributed in the United Kingdom by GMC Distribution Services,
Castle Place, 166 High Street, Lewes, East Sussex, England BN7 1XU
Distributed in Australia by Capricorn Link (Australia) Pty. Ltd.,
P.O. Box 704, Windsor, NSW 2756, Australia
Printed in China. All rights reserved.
Sterling ISBN-13: 978-1-4027-2224-0
ISBN-10: 1-4027-2224-9

For information about custom editions, special sales, premium and
corporate purchases, please contact Sterling Special Sales
Department at 800-805-5489 or specialsales@sterlingpub.com.

Avery kicked the toe of his boot in the dirt. He looked at everyone else at Cowboy Camp and knew he was all wrong. His belt buckle was too big. His hat was too small. His boots were too red. Even his name was wrong. The other boys had tough names, like Hank or Jimmy Jean. *Whoever heard of a cowboy named Avery?* he thought.

"Howdy, y'all. I'm Cowboy Dan, and I'm about to turn you little ragamuffins into cowboys. Real cowboys," said the realest looking cowboy Avery had ever seen. "By the time I finish with you, you'll be actin', walkin', and talkin' like honest-to-goodness cowboys. First things first, though, buckaroos. It's chow time. There's enough grits and beans here to give y'all a bellyache."

Everyone dug in. It wasn't but a minute later that Avery
discovered he couldn't stomach a single bite of cowboy food.
He had to eat cheese and crackers instead. *Whoever heard of
a cowboy who didn't like grits and beans?* he thought.

"Now that you've got your fill, it's horse ridin' time,"
Cowboy Dan announced. "Let's hit the stables."

Everyone saddled up. It wasn't but a minute later that Avery discovered he was allergic to horses. "Ah-ah-ah-CHOOOOO!" sneezed Avery as he climbed onto his horse.

He had to ride a cow instead. *Whoever heard of a cowboy who was allergic to horses?* he thought.

"All right, fellas, it's time to round up some cattle. Let me teach y'all how to lasso," Cowboy Dan said.

Everyone started twistin' and twirlin' their lassos. It wasn't but a minute later that Avery discovered he had a bad case of rope burn. He had to practice with yarn instead. *Whoever heard of a cowboy who got rope burn?* he thought.

That night, after all the other cowboy campers turned in for some shut-eye, Avery sat outside his tent and tried to think cowboy thoughts. It wasn't but a minute later that Avery discovered he wasn't alone. Out of the shadows stepped the meanest looking cowboy Avery had ever seen.

"Kid. *Pssst.* Kid," a gruff voice said.

"Who, me?" asked Avery.

"Yeah, you. I'm Black Bart and I'm here to put a stop to Cowboy Camp. Cowboy Dan and his gangs of good cowboys are makin' it too hard to be a bad guy. You better tell me, kid—where can I find Cowboy Dan?"

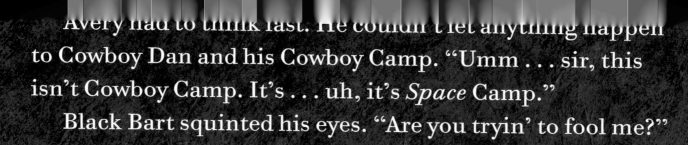

Avery had to think fast. He couldn't let anything happen to Cowboy Dan and his Cowboy Camp. "Umm . . . sir, this isn't Cowboy Camp. It's . . . uh, it's *Space* Camp."

Black Bart squinted his eyes. "Are you tryin' to fool me?"

"Sir," asked Avery, "do I *look* like cowboy material?"

Black Bart took a step back and sized Avery up. "I dunno, but I aim to find out. Here, eat this." Black Bart pulled a can of beans out of his saddlebag. "*All* cowboys eat beans."

Avery gulped. He took the beans and gave them
a taste. Right away he coughed and wheezed.

"Hmm . . . maybe you ain't a cowboy. You don't seem to like cowboy food," said Black Bart. "Let me see you ride my horse. *All* cowboys ride horses."

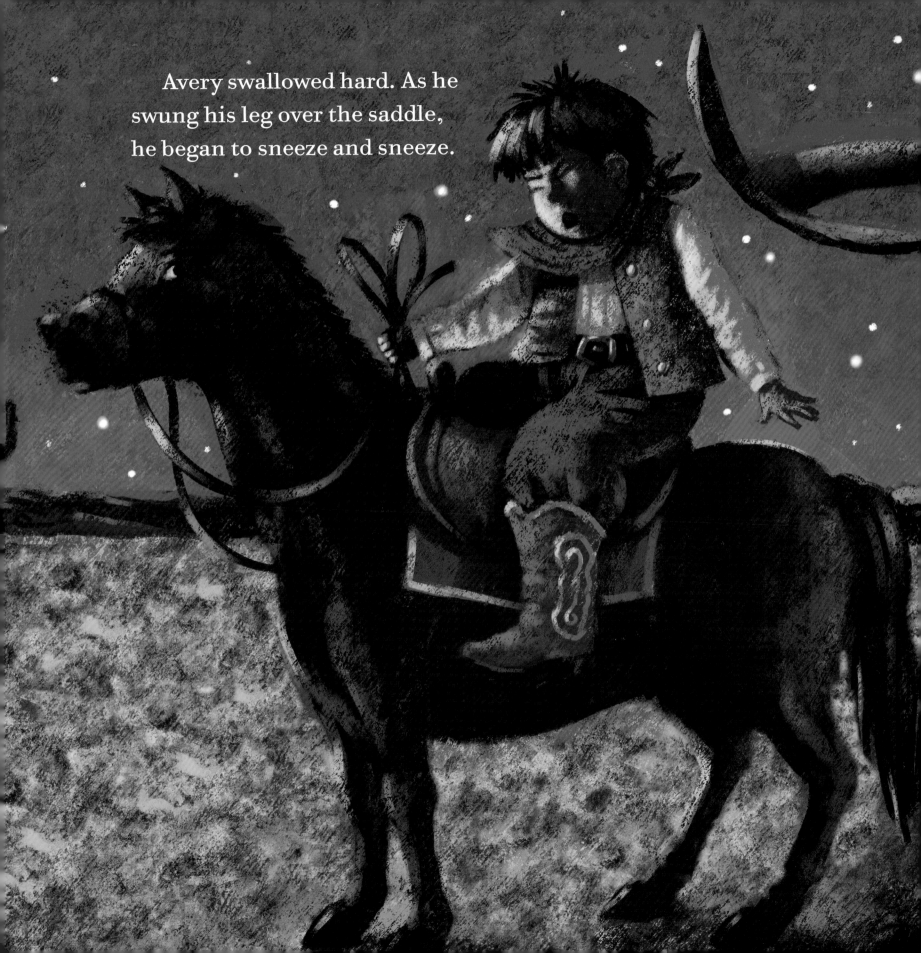

Avery swallowed hard. As he swung his leg over the saddle, he began to sneeze and sneeze.

"Hmm . . . maybe you ain't a cowboy. You don't seem to ride horses," said Black Bart. "Let me see you twirl my rope. *All* cowboys know how to lasso."

Avery took a deep breath. As he grabbed the rope, he yelped, "Ouch, this hurts!"

"Little feller, you're no cowboy. All cowboys eat beans, ride horses, and twirl lassos. This place can't possibly be Cowboy Camp," Black Bart said. "Rustlin' rattlesnakes! I musta made a wrong turn somewhere. I gotta go. It'll be daybreak soon and time's a wastin'."

It wasn't but a minute later that Cowboy Dan and the other cowboy campers came out of their tents.

"Avery, you're about the bravest durn cowboy I ever laid eyes on," said Cowboy Dan. "No one but a real cowboy could outsmart the likes of Black Bart the way you just did."

Avery grinned. His smile was as bright as his too-big belt buckle. He felt brave. He felt amazing. He felt like a real honest-to-goodness cowboy.